BULSTRODE

Based on *The Railway Series*

Illustrations by
Robin Davies and Jerry Smith

EGMONT

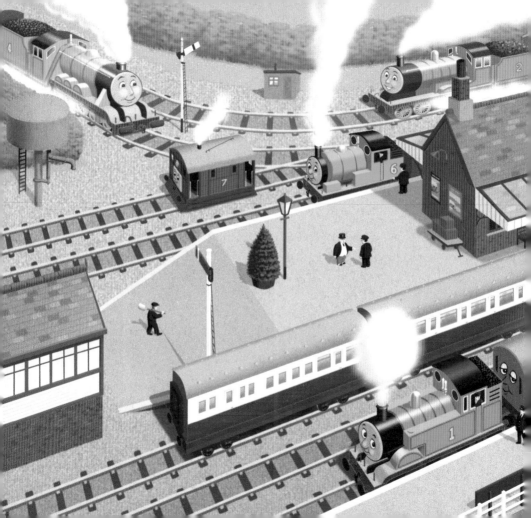

First published in Great Britain 2004
by Egmont Books Limited
239 Kensington High Street, London W8 6SA
All Rights Reserved

Thomas the Tank Engine & Friends

A BRITT ALLCROFT COMPANY PRODUCTION

Based on The Railway Series by The Rev W Awdry

ISBN 1 4052 1039 7
7 9 10 8
Printed in Great Britain

This is a story about Bulstrode the Barge. He was a very disagreeable barge who was always causing trouble. Then one day, he went too far …

One morning, Percy was shunting trucks in the yard. The trucks were being very naughty and refusing to move.

"Come on! Come on!" puffed Percy as he pushed them into place.

"Oh! Oh! Oh!" screamed the trucks as they bumped into each other.

Just as Percy was about to give them one last big push, The Fat Controller arrived.

"Leave those trucks please, Percy," said The Fat Controller. "There's an emergency at the Harbour!"

"Yes, Sir," replied Percy, happily. He was pleased that he could leave the naughty trucks behind.

"Come on, Percy," said his Driver. "This will be trouble with Bulstrode."

Percy had never met Bulstrode and wondered what kind of engine he would be.

As they puffed along the line, Percy's Driver told him all about Bulstrode.

"Bulstrode isn't an engine. He is a very disagreeable barge," his Driver explained. "He never stops complaining and always expects everyone to do what he wants."

Percy hadn't met a barge before, but he wasn't looking forward to meeting Bulstrode.

Percy's Driver was right about Bulstrode. Today, the barge was more bad-tempered than ever. At the Harbour, he was shouting at the trucks.

"Come on, come on. Why aren't you trucks where you should be?" complained Bulstrode.

"There's no engine and we can't move without one," replied the trucks. "You're in the wrong place, not us."

Bulstrode and the trucks had been arguing all morning. The trucks had some coal for Bulstrode to deliver, but they were too far away from the water to load him up.

Bulstrode was being very impatient. He didn't want to wait for an engine to arrive.

When Percy arrived, Bulstrode was sulking, and the trucks were even more angry than before.

"Bulstrode is being difficult," complained the trucks. "Please put us in a siding, Percy, so that we can load him up and be rid of him!"

"Rid of me?" replied Bulstrode. "I would have left hours ago if you trucks were in the right place."

Percy wasn't happy that he had to shunt trucks again. But he was unhappier still about the way Bulstrode spoke to him!

"Pah! Look at the size of you!" laughed Bulstrode. "I'd be surprised if you had the strength to move even one truck!"

Percy didn't like Bulstrode. He wanted to get the job done as quickly as possible.

Percy began to move the trucks. But the trucks were being careless. As Percy lined them up, they burst through some buffers.

The trucks screamed and laughed as they hurtled towards the edge of the dock. But it was too late. Bulstrode could see them coming towards him! And before anyone had time to stop them, the trucks went over the edge of the dock!

"Oooof!" cried Bulstrode, as the trucks landed on him. "I'm sinking!"

"Serves you right," giggled the trucks. "You were always barging in and moaning!"

"Blah ..." replied Bulstrode. His mouth was full of coal!

"Ha! Ha!" giggled the trucks. "You don't have anything clever to say now!"

Percy smiled. He thought Bulstrode had got what he deserved.

The Harbour was a terrible mess. There was coal everywhere and half the trucks were on Bulstrode instead of the track! It took a very long time to clear the mess up.

Cranky the Crane had to lift the trucks out of Bulstrode one by one. The trucks giggled and teased Bulstrode. But Bulstrode was surprisingly quiet.

Percy watched as Bulstrode was towed away to the beach. He had caused trouble one too many times.

"Right," said the workmen, when they reached the beach. "You can stay here from now on. Children can play in you all day and at long last you'll be useful."

"You can't leave me here!" shouted Bulstrode. But the workmen ignored him and walked away.

As Percy puffed along the line to The Fat Controller's Railway, he passed Bulstrode on the beach. Bulstrode was already shouting at the seagulls that had perched on top of him. Percy hurried past, before Bulstrode had a chance to shout at him!

"I'm so pleased that I won't have to work with Bulstrode again," thought Percy, when he was safely out of his way. "The Troublesome Trucks are naughty, but Bulstrode is even worse!"

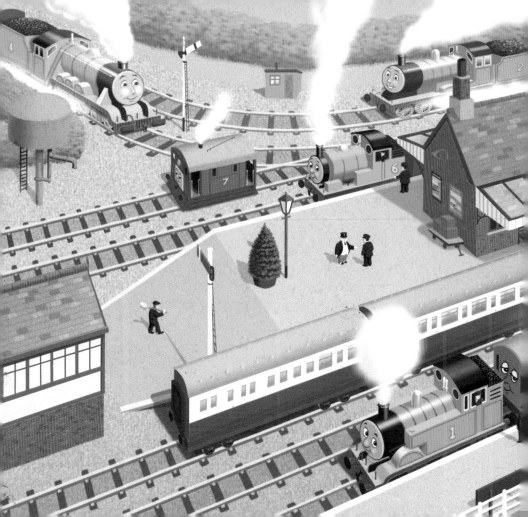

The Thomas Story Library is THE definitive collection of stories about Thomas and ALL his Friends.

5 more Thomas Story Library titles will be chuffing into your local bookshop in Summer 2006:

Fergus
Mighty Mac
Harvey
Rusty
Molly

And there are even more
Thomas Story Library books to follow later!
So go on, start your Thomas Story Library NOW!

A Fantastic Offer for Thomas the Tank Engine Fans!

In every Thomas Story Library book like this one, you will find a special token. Collect 6 Thomas tokens and we will send you a brilliant Thomas poster, and a double-sided bedroom door hanger!

Simply tape a £1 coin in the space above, and fill out the form overleaf.

TO BE COMPLETED BY AN ADULT

To apply for this great offer, ask an adult to complete the coupon below and send it with a pound coin and 6 tokens, to:
THOMAS OFFERS, PO BOX 715, HORSHAM RH12 5WG

☐ Please send a Thomas poster and door hanger. I enclose 6 tokens plus a £1 coin. (Price includes P&P)

Fan's name...

Address..

....Postcode..................................

Date of birth...

Name of parent/guardian...

Signature of parent/guardian..

Please allow 28 days for delivery. Offer is only available while stocks last. We reserve the right to change the terms of this offer at any time and we offer a 14 day money back guarantee. This does not affect your statutory rights.

☐ Data Protection Act: If you do not wish to receive other similar offers from us or companies we recommend, please tick this box. Offers apply to UK only.